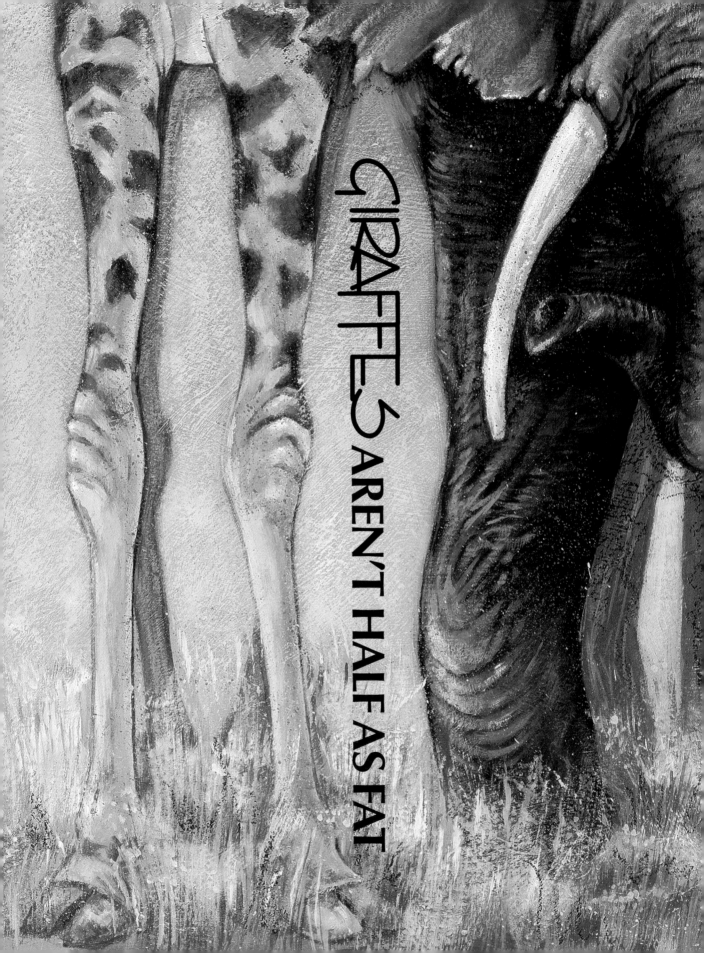

GIRAFFES AREN'T HALF AS FAT

GIRAFFES

AREN'T HALF AS FAT

BY MIRIAM ARONER
Illustrations by
Mary Newell DePalma

The Millbrook Press
Brookfield, Connecticut

TO MY BEAUTIFUL CHILDREN, JONATHAN AND SARAH
M.A.

TO MOM AND DAD, WITH LOVE
M.N.D.

Library of Congress Cataloging-in-Publication Data
Aroner, Miriam.
Giraffes aren't half as fat / by Miriam Aroner ;
illustrations by Mary Newell DePalma.
p.   cm.
ISBN 1-56294-484-3 (lib. bdg.)   ISBN 1-56294-884-9 (tr.)
1. Giraffes—Juvenile literature.   [1. Giraffes.]
I. DePalma, Mary Newell, ill.   II. Title.
QL737. U56A78 1995 599.73'57—dc20 94-2046 CIP AC

Published by The Millbrook Press
2 Old New Milford Road, Brookfield, Connecticut 06804

Text copyright © 1995 by Miriam Aroner
Illustrations © 1995 by Mary Newell DePalma
All rights reserved
Printed in the United States of America
1 3 5 4 2

Giraffes aren't half as fat
as elephants.
They're so tall, next to them
all other animals look small.
At birth giraffes are six feet tall,
and by age four almost full-grown.

Their necks go so high
no creature can see
eye-to-eye with giraffes.
But giraffes can see
far beyond the tops of trees—
Uh oh! A lion's on the prowl!

Spots are spots, you may say.
But each giraffe has its own special spots
arranged in its own special way.
Can you "spot" giraffes
hiding in the trees?

When danger's past,
with a whish of a tail
or a flick of an ear
a giraffe says "I'm here!"

Giraffes can doze standing up.
But sometimes they nap lying down.
They rest their heads upon their backs
and fold their legs into a heap, and sleep.
When they wake,
they wiggle and wobble to stand.

Giraffes never take baths.
They hate to get wet.
They can't swim, and it's hard to bend.
So they lick themselves clean
with their long, long tongues.

When giraffes want to drink
they have to be wary.
With front legs spread
and heads lower than necks,
giraffes can't move fast.

If a lion comes near—
Oh dear!
Giraffes on a tilt need to worry!

So, quickly they sip
and keep looking around
in case they must leave in a hurry!

Giraffes like to hang around in herds.
"Uncles" fight, but in a playful way,
nuzzling necks and bumping heads.
They keep watch when others are asleep.
"Aunties" tend the calves
while the mothers search for lunch.

Giraffes love treetop salad.
They gobble the leaves of the acacia,
their favorite food.
Fruits and berries, blossoms and twigs
all make a delicious meal.

In Africa, their home,
giraffes are free to roam.
They live in peace with other beasts
(except the lion).

If you can't go to Africa
you can visit giraffes in the zoo.
Look up at their beautiful faces.
Are they watching you?

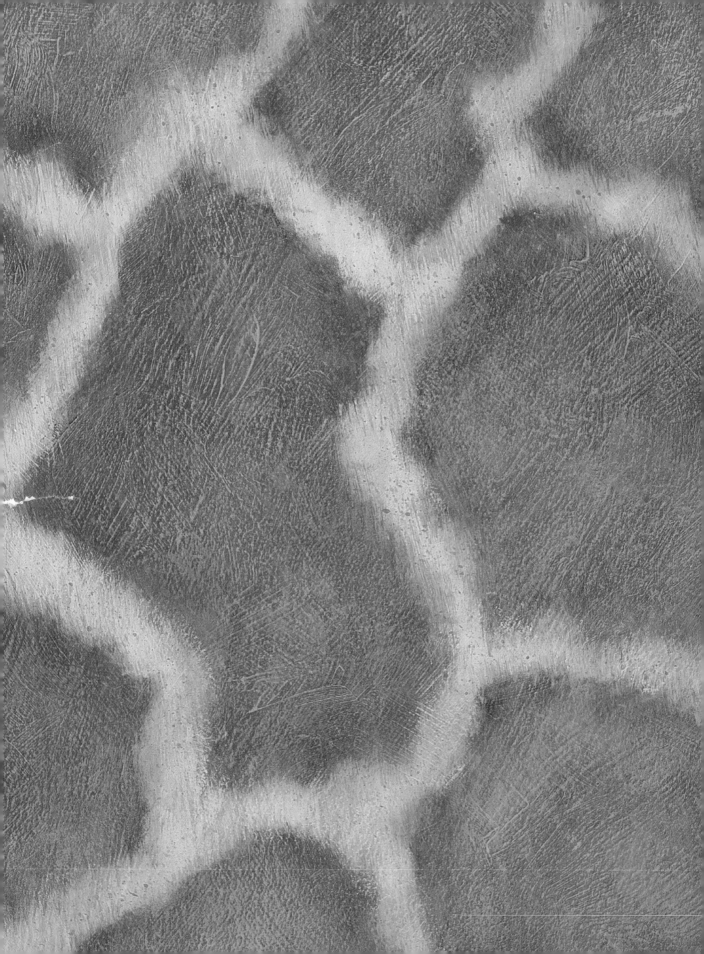

Facts About Giraffes

How big are giraffes?

Other animals may weigh more. An elephant may weigh five times as much as a giraffe! But giraffes are the tallest animals in the world. A full-grown male is 18 feet (5.5 meters) tall and weighs up to 3,000 pounds (more than 1,350 kilograms). Females are almost as big.

Where do giraffes live?

Giraffes are found in Africa, south of the Sahara desert. They prefer open, brushy areas. Today farms and towns cover many areas where giraffes once lived. Most giraffes live in parks and preserves.

What do giraffes eat and drink?

Giraffes are herbivores—they eat only plants. Acacia leaves, their favorite food, also provide them with some water. This helps them go for days without drinking; if necessary, they can survive for a week without water.

How do giraffes eat?

They digest their food in a special way. The giraffe strips leaves from trees with its long black tongue and swallows its food quickly, without chewing. Like cows, giraffes have a four-part stomach. The food mixes with digestive juices in the first part of the stomach and forms into lumps, or cuds, in the second. The cuds are brought back up to the mouth and chewed slowly. This is called rumination. Then the cuds are swallowed again and fully digested.

Do giraffes make sounds?

Many people think giraffes are silent. But giraffes sometimes grunt or bleat, and they may make sounds we can't hear.

How are baby giraffes born?

Like other mammals, giraffes are born live. The female carries the calf for 14 to 15 months. Then she gives birth standing up, and the calf drops gently to the ground. It already weighs about 150 pounds (almost 70 kilograms). Within an hour or so, it can walk.

How big are giraffe herds?

Giraffes usually form small groups of two to ten animals. Many groups are formed by females and calves.

Do all giraffes have horns?

All giraffes have at least two horns; some have four or five. Males' horns are twice as long as females' horns. The horns are used in friendly sparring, mostly by males. They are covered by skin, but the ends often look bare because this sparring wears off their hairs.

Do giraffes have enemies?

Giraffes' main enemies are lions, who kill them for food, and humans, who kill them for food, for their skins, or for sport. Giraffes defend themselves against lions by kicking with their powerful legs. They have few defenses against humans. But some African countries have taken steps to protect giraffes. They have passed laws making it illegal to kill giraffes and have set up parks and preserves where giraffes can live safely.

About the Author and Artist

Miriam Aroner's previous books for young readers include *The Kingdom of Singing Birds*. A member of the Society of Children's Book Writers and Illustrators, she holds advanced degrees in English and library science. She lives in El Cerrito, California.

Mary Newell DePalma's many illustration credits range from a version of the classic tale *Goldilocks and the Three Bears* to classroom materials and conservation literature. A native of Pittsburgh, Pennsylvania, she holds a degree in medical illustration from Rochester Institute of Technology and lives in Boston, Massachusetts.